Alexander McCal^l Smith

Precious and
the Monkeys

Alexander McCall Smith was born in Africa but now lives in Scotland. He is the author of over eighty books, including the best-selling No.1 Ladies' Detective series. He writes for children with as much pleasure as he writes for adults.

Iain McIntosh's illustrations have won numerous awards in the worlds of design, advertising and books. He lives and works in the New Town of Edinburgh, close to 44 Scotland Street.

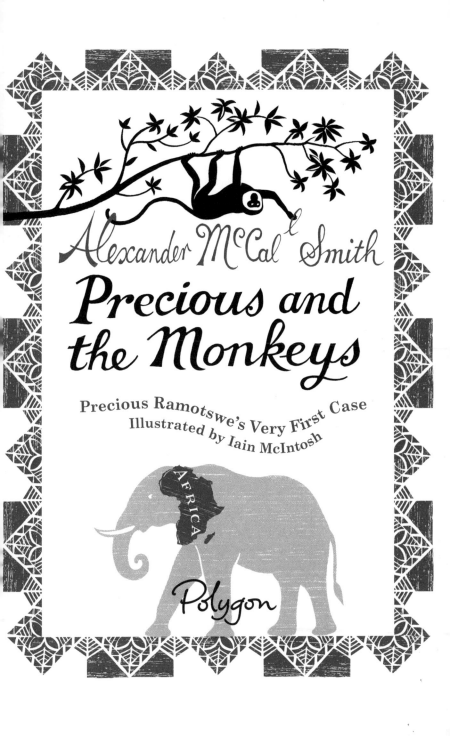

Alexander McCall Smith

Precious and the Monkeys

Precious Ramotswe's Very First Case
Illustrated by Iain McIntosh

Polygon

This edition first published in 2014 by

Polygon, an imprint of Birlinn Ltd
West Newington House
10 Newington Road
Edinburgh
EH9 1QS

www.polygonbooks.co.uk

9 8 7 6 5 4 3 2 1

ISBN 978-1-84697-320-8

First published in the Scots language in 2010
by Itchy Coo

Printed and bound in Latvia
by Livonia Print

INTRODUCTION

A number of years ago I went to live for a short time in a country called Botswana. This is a very beautiful country in Africa – a place famous for its great wild places and the animals that live in them. When I lived there, I remember thinking: it would be fun to write about this place some day.

And I did. A long time afterwards, I sat down one day and wrote a story about a lady called Precious Ramotswe, who lives in Botswana, and who starts a little business. People thought that she might start a small store or something like that, but instead she sets up a detective agency. A detective agency! What does she know about being a detective? The answer to that is nothing, but – and this is an important but – she has just the right talents for it. She is a born detective – which means that she is somebody who is naturally good at the work involved in being a detective.

She is not one of those police detectives who solve major crimes. No, she is a person who deals with the mysteries that ordinary people – just like you and me – may have in their lives. So if we think that somebody is not telling us the truth about something, then we may go to her and ask her to find out what is really going on. Or if we have lost something that is very important to us, we may ask her to find it. Such people are called private detectives.

I have now written quite a number of books about Precious Ramotswe and from time to time, people have asked me more about her life. One of the questions I have been asked is this: what was Precious like as a girl? That is what this book is about.

Although there is no actual Precious Ramotswe in real life, I can promise you that there are plenty of girls and women in Botswana who are just like her. I have met lots of ladies – and girls too – in that country who are every bit as intelligent and kind and nice as Precious Ramotswe is. And Botswana is real, as is the village of Mochudi, which is where she lives. So yes, it could be true – she really could exist.

That's enough from me. Now listen to the story. Think of Africa. Think of a girl living there. Think of what it would be like to discover, when you are still quite young, that you are a born detective ...

ALEXANDER McCALL SMITH

A MAP OF
BOTSWANA

PULA

OKAVANGO

KALAHARI
DESERT

Francistown

BOTSWANA

0 miles 100

GABORONE

HAVE YOU EVER SAID TO YOURSELF – not out loud, of course, but silently, just in your head: *Wouldn't it be nice to be a detective?* I have, and so have a lot of other people, although most of us will never have the chance to make our dream come true. Detectives, you see, are born that way. Right from the beginning, they just *know* that this is what they want to be. And right from the beginning, even when they are very young – a lot younger than you – they show that solving mysteries is something they can do rather well.

This is the story of a girl who became a detective. Her first name was Precious, and her second name was Ramotswe.

RAM ● OTS ● WE

That is an African name, and it is not as hard to say it as it looks. You just say RAM and then you say OTS (like *lots* without the l) and then you finish it off by saying WE. That's it.

This is a picture of Precious when she was about seven. She is smiling because she was thinking at the time of something funny, although she often smiled even when she was not thinking about anything in particular. Nice people smile a lot, and Precious Ramotswe was one of the nicest girls in Botswana. Everyone said that.

Botswana was the country she lived in. It was down towards the bottom of Africa, right in the middle. This meant that it was very far from the sea. Precious had never seen the sea, although she had heard people talk about it.

"The sound of the waves is like the sound of a high wind in the branches of the trees," people said. "It's like that sound, but it never stops."

She would have loved to stand beside the sea, and to let the waves wash over her toes, but it was too far away for her wish to be granted. So she had to content herself with the wide dry land that she lived in, which had a lot of amazing things to see anyway.

There was the Kalahari Desert, a great stretch of dry grass and thorn trees that went on and on into the distance, further than any eye can see. Then there was the great river in the north, which flowed the wrong way, not into the ocean, as rivers usually do, but back into the heart of Africa. When it reached the sands of the Kalahari, it drained away, just like water disappears down the plughole of a bath.

But most exciting, of course, were the wild animals. There were many of these in Botswana: lions, elephants, leopards, ostriches, monkeys – the list goes on and on. Precious had not seen all of these animals, but she had heard about most of them. Her father, a kind man whose name was Obed, had often spoken about them, and she loved the tales he told.

"Tell me about the time you were nearly eaten by a lion," she would ask. And Obed, who had told her that story perhaps a hundred times before, would tell her again. And it was every bit as exciting each time he told it.

"I was quite young then," he began.

"How young?" asked Precious.

"About eighteen, I think," he said. "It was just before I went off to work in the gold mines. I went up north to see my uncle, who lived way out in the bush, very far from everywhere."

"Did anybody else live there?" asked Precious. She was always asking questions, which was a sign that she might become a detective later on. Many people who ask lots of questions become detectives, because that is what detectives have to do.

"It was a very small village," said Obed. "It was just a few huts, really, and a fenced place where they kept the cattle. They had this fence, you see, which protected the cattle from the lions at night."

As you can imagine, this fence had to be quite strong. You cannot keep lions out with a fence that is no more than a few strands of wire. That is hopeless when it comes to lions – they would just knock down such a fence with a single blow of their paw. A proper lion fence has to be made of strong poles, from the trunks of trees, just like this:

That is a good, solid lion fence.

"So there I was," Obed went on. "I had gone to spend a few days with my uncle and his family. They were good to me and I enjoyed being with my cousins, whom I had not seen for a long time. There were six of them – four boys and two girls. We had many adventures together.

"I slept in one of the huts with three of the boys. We did not have proper beds in those days – we had sleeping mats, made out of reeds, which we laid out on the floor of the hut. They were very comfortable, even if it doesn't sound like it, and they were much cooler than a bed and blankets in the hot weather, and easier to store too."

Precious was quiet now. This was the part of the story that she was waiting for.

"And then," her father continued, "and then one night I woke up to hear a strange sound outside. It was a sort of grunting sound, a little bit like the sound a large pig will make when it's sniffing about for food, only deeper."

"Did you know what it was?" she asked, holding her breath as she waited for her father to reply. She knew what the answer would be, of course, as she had heard the story so many times, but it was always exciting, always enough to keep you sitting on the very edge of your seat.

He shook his head. "No, I didn't. And that was why I thought I should go outside and find out."

Precious closed her eyes tight, just like this. She could hardly bear to hear what was coming.

"It was a lion," said her father. "And he was right outside the hut, standing there, looking at me in the night from underneath his great, dark mane."

Like this.

Precious opened her eyes cautiously, one at a time, just in case there was a lion in the room. But there was just her father, telling his story.

"How did that lion get in?" she asked. "How did he get past that big strong fence?"

Obed shook his head. "I later found out that somebody had not fastened the gate properly," he said. "It was carelessness."

But enough of that. It was time to get on with the story of what happened next.

HAT WOULD YOU DO if you found
yourself face to face with a great
lion? Stand perfectly still? Turn on
your heels and run? Creep quietly
away? Perhaps you would just close your
eyes and hope that you were dreaming –
which is what Obed did at first when he
saw the terrifying lion staring straight at
him. But when he opened his eyes again,
the lion was still there, and worse still, was
beginning to open his great mouth.

Precious caught her breath. "Did you
see his teeth?" she asked.

Obed nodded. "The moonlight was very
bright," he said. "His teeth were white and
as sharp as great needles."

Precious shuddered at the thought, and listened intently as her father explained what happened next.

Obed moved his head very slowly – not enough to alarm the lion, but just enough for him to look for escape routes. He could not get back to the hut, he thought, as it would take him too close to the frightening beast. Off to his left, though, just a few paces away, were the family's grain bins. These were large bins, rather like garden pots – but much bigger – that were used for storing the maize that the family grew for their food. They were made out of pressed mud, baked hard by the hot sun, and were very strong.

Obed lowered his voice. "I looked up at the night sky and thought, *I'll never see the sun again.* And then I looked down at the ground and thought, *I'll never feel my beloved Botswana under my feet again.* But the next thing I said to myself was, *No, I must do something. I must not let this lion eat me!*

"I made up my mind and ran – not back to the hut, but to the nearest grain bin. I pushed the cover back and jumped in, bringing the lid down on top of my head. I was safe!"

Precious breathed a sigh of relief. But she knew that there was more to come.

"There was very little grain left in that bin," Obed went on. "There were just a few husks and dusty bits. So there was plenty of room for me to crouch down."

"And spiders too?" asked Precious, with a shudder.

"There are always spiders in grain bins," said Obed. "But it wasn't spiders I was worried about."

"It was …"

Obed finished the sentence for her. "Yes, it was the lion. He had been a bit surprised when I jumped into the bin, and now I could hear him outside, scratching and snuffling at the lid.

"I knew that it would only be a matter of time before he pushed the lid off with one of his great paws, and I knew that I had to do something. But what could I do?"

Precious knew the answer. "You could take some of the dusty bits and pieces from the bottom of the bin and …"

Obed laughed. "Exactly. And that's what I did. I took a handful of those dusty husks and then, pushing up the lid a tiny bit, I tossed them straight into the face of the inquisitive lion."

Precious looked at her father wide-eyed. She knew that this was the good part of the story.

"And what did he do?" she asked.

Obed smiled. "He was very surprised," he said. "He breathed them in and then he gave the loudest, most amazing, most powerful sneeze that has ever been sneezed in Botswana, or possibly in all Africa. Ka… chow! Like this.

"It was a very great sneeze," Obed said. "It was a sneeze that was heard from miles away, and it was certainly heard by everybody in the village. In every hut, people awoke, rubbed their eyes, and rose from their sleeping mats. 'A great lion has sneezed,' they said to one another. 'We must all hit our pots and pans as hard as we can. That will frighten him away.' "

And that is what happened. As the people began to strike their pots and pans with spoons and forks and anything else that came to hand, the lion tucked his tail between his legs and ran off into the bush. He was not frightened of eating one unfortunate young man, but even he could not stand up to a whole village of people all making a terrible din. Lions do not usually like that sort of thing, and this one certainly did not.

"I am glad that you were not eaten by that lion," said Precious.

"And so am I," said Obed.

"Because if the lion had eaten you, I would never have been born," Precious said.

"And if you had never been born, then I would never have been able to get to know the brightest and nicest girl in all Botswana," said her father.

Precious thought for a moment. "So it would have been a bad thing for both of us," she said at last.

"Yes," said Obed. "And maybe a bad thing for the lion too."

"Oh, why was that?"

"Because I might have given him indigestion," said Obed. "It's a well-known fact that if a lion eats a person who's feeling cross at the time, he gets indigestion."

Precious looked at her father suspiciously. She was not sure whether this was true, or whether he was just making it up to amuse her. She decided that it was not true, and told him so.

He smiled, and looked at her in a curious way. "You can tell when people are making things up, can't you?"

Precious nodded. She thought that was probably right – she *could* tell.

"Perhaps you should become a detective one day," he said.

And that was how the idea of becoming a detective was first planted in the mind of Precious Ramotswe, who was still only seven, but who was about to embark on a career as Botswana's greatest detective!

ETECTIVES sometimes say to one another: it's your first case that's always the hardest. Well, Precious was never sure if that was true for her, but her first case was certainly not easy.

It happened not long after her father had told her that one day she might become a detective. When he said that, she had at first thought *What a strange idea*, but then she asked herself, *Why not?* That's often what you think after somebody makes an odd suggestion. *Why not?* And after you've asked that question, you think *Well, yes!* And then you decide that there really is no reason why you shouldn't do it.

Not always, of course. If somebody suggests something stupid, or unkind, then you should quickly see all the reasons why not. And then you say, *No thank you!* Or *Certainly not!* Or something of that sort.

But Precious said to herself, "Yes, I could be a detective. But surely it will be years and years before I get a case."

She was wrong about that. A case came
up sooner than she thought. This is what
happened.

The school Precious went to was on a
hill. This meant that children had quite a
climb in the mornings, but once they were
up there, what a wonderful place it was for
their lessons. Looking out of the windows,

they could gaze out to where other little hills popped up like islands in the sea. And you could hear sounds from far away too – the tinkling of cattle bells, the rumbling of thunder in the distance, the cry of a bird of prey soaring in the wind.

It was, as you can imagine, a very happy school. The teachers were happy to be working in such a nice town, the children

were happy to have kind teachers who did not shout at them too much, and even the school cat, who had a comfortable den outside, was happy with the mice that could be chased most days.

But then something nasty happened. That is what the world is sometimes like: everything seems fine, and then something happens to spoil things.

What happened was that there was a thief. Now, most people don't steal things. Most people – and that certainly includes you and me – know that things that belong to other people belong to other people. For many of us, that is Rule Number One, and sometimes you see it written out like this:

RULE NUMBER ONE
Don't help yourself to other people's things!

And Rule Number Two? Well that's another matter altogether, and we all know what it is anyway. So, a thief ... and a thief at school too!

The first person to notice what was going on was Tapiwa (TAP-EE-WAH) a girl in the same class as Precious.

TAP◆EE◆WAH

"Do you know what?" she whispered to Precious as they made their way home after school one afternoon.

"No," said Precious. "What?"

"There must be a thief at school," said Tapiwa, looking over her shoulder in case anybody heard what she had to say. "I brought a piece of cake to school with me this morning. I left it in my bag in the corridor outside the classroom." She paused before she went on. "I was really looking forward to eating it at break-time."

"I love cake," said Precious, closing her eyes and thinking of some of the cakes she had enjoyed. Iced cakes. Cakes with jam on top of them. Cakes sprinkled with sugar and then dipped in little coloured sugar-balls. There were so many cakes ... and all of them were so delicious.

"Somebody took my cake," Tapiwa complained. "I had wrapped it in a small piece of paper. Well, it was gone, and I found the paper lying on the floor."

Precious frowned. "Gone?"

"Eaten up," said Tapiwa. "There were crumbs on the floor and little bits of icing. I picked them up and tasted them. I could tell that they came from my cake."

"Did you tell the teacher?" asked Precious.

Her friend sighed. "Yes," she said. "But I don't think that she believed me. She said, 'Are you sure you didn't forget that you ate it?' She said that this sometimes happened. People ate a piece of cake and then forgot that they had done so."

Precious gazed at Tapiwa. Was she the sort of person to eat a piece of cake and then forget all about it? She did not think so.

"It was stolen," said Tapiwa. "That's what happened. There's a thief in the school. Who do you think it is?"

"I don't know," said Precious. She found it hard to imagine any member of their class doing something like that. Everybody seemed so honest. And yet, when you came to think of it, if there were grown-up thieves, then those thieves must have been children once, and perhaps they were already thieves even when they were young. Or did people only become thieves a bit later on, when they turned sixteen or something like that? It was a very interesting question, and she would have

to think about it a bit more. Which is what
she did as she walked home that day, under
that high, hot African sun. She thought
about thieves and what to do about them.

IT MIGHT HAVE BEEN EASY for her to forget about it – after all, it was only a piece of cake – but the next day it happened again. This time it was a piece of bread that was stolen – not an ordinary piece of bread, though: this one was covered in delicious red jam. You can lose a plain piece of bread and not think twice about it, but when you lose one spread thickly with red jam it's an altogether more serious matter.

The owner of this piece of bread (with jam) was a small boy called Sepo. Everybody liked this boy because he had a habit of saying funny things. And people like that, because there are enough sad

31

things in the world as it is. If somebody can say something funny, then that often makes everybody feel a bit better. Try it yourself: say something funny and see how pleased everybody is.

This is a picture of Sepo.

You will see that he is smiling. And this is a picture of the piece of bread and red jam. Yes, if you saw such

a piece of bread sitting on a plate your mouth would surely begin to water. And yes, you might imagine how delicious it would taste. But would you really eat it if you knew it belonged to somebody else?

Of course not.

It happened at lunch-time. Every day, at twelve o'clock precisely, the school cook, a very large lady called Mma Molipi (MO-

MO·LEE·PEE

LEE -PEE), always called Big Mma Molipi, would bang a saucepan with a ladle. This was the signal for all the children to sit down on the verandah and wait to be given a plate of food that she had cooked with her assistant and cousin. This assistant was called Not-so-Big Mma Molipi, and,

as the name tells us, she was much smaller than the chief cook herself. This is a picture of the two of them standing together. You will see how different they are.

"Time for lunch!" Big Mma Molipi would shout in her very loud voice.

Then Not-so-Big Mma Molipi would shout, in a much smaller, squeakier voice, "Time for lunch!"

Big Mma Molipi's food was all right, but not all that all right. It was, in fact, a bit boring, as she only had one recipe, it seemed, which was a sort of paste made out of corn and served with green peas and mashed turnips.

Dinner time!

"It's very healthy," said Big Mma Molipi. "So stop complaining, children, and eat up!"

34

"Yes," said Not-so-Big Mma Molipi. "So stop complaining, children, and eat up!"

As you can see, Not-so-Big Mma Molipi did not say anything other than what she heard her larger cousin say. She thought it was safer that way. If you said anything new, she imagined, then people could look at you, and Not-so-Big Mma Molipi did not like the thought of that.

It was no surprise that many of the children liked to make lunch a little bit more interesting by bringing their own food. Some brought a bit of fruit, or a sugar doughnut, or perhaps a sweet biscuit.

Then, after lunch, when they all had a bit of free time before going back into the classroom, they would eat these special treats. Or, if they had nothing to bring, they could watch other people eating theirs. Sometimes, when you are very hungry, it's the next best thing just to watch other people eating. But this can also make you even hungrier, unless you are careful.

Sepo had brought his piece of bread and jam in a brown paper bag. While Big Mma Molipi served lunch, he had left the bag in

the classroom, tucked away safely under his desk. He was sure that this is where he left it, and so when he went back in and saw that it had disappeared he was very surprised indeed.

"My bread!" he wailed. "Somebody's taken my bread!"

Precious was walking past the open door of the classroom when she heard this. She looked in; there was Sepo standing miserably by his desk.

"Are you sure?" Precious asked.

"Of course I'm sure," said Sepo. "It was there when we went out for lunch. Now it isn't, and I didn't take it."

Precious went into the classroom and stared at the spot being pointed out by Sepo. There was certainly nothing there.

"I'll ask people if they saw anything," she said. "In the meantime, you can have half of my biscuit. I hope that will make you feel better."

It did. Sepo was still upset, but not quite as upset as he had been when he made the discovery.

"There must be a thief in the school," said Sepo as they walked out into the playground. "Who do you think it is, Precious?"

Precious shrugged. "I just don't know," she said. "It could be ..." She paused. "It could be anyone."

Sepo looked thoughtful. "I think I may know who it is," he said. He did not speak very loudly, even though there was nobody else about.

Precious looked at him quizzically. "How do you know that? Did you see somebody taking it?"

Sepo looked furtively over his shoulder. "No," he said. "I didn't see anybody actually take it. But I did see somebody walking away from the classroom door."

Precious held her breath, waiting for

Sepo to say more. He stayed silent, though, and so she whispered to him, "Who?"

Sepo did not say anything, but after hesitating for a moment or two he very carefully pointed to somebody standing in the playground.

"Him," he whispered. "It's him. I saw him."

Precious frowned. "Are you sure?" she asked.

Sepo thought for a moment. If you ask somebody what they saw, they often have to think for a while before they answer. And they often get it wrong. But now Sepo said, "I'm sure – I really am. And look at him. Don't you think that he *looks* as if he's been eating too much!"

"Don't say anything," said Precious. "You can't accuse another person of doing something unless you actually saw it happen."

Sepo looked doubtful. "Why not?" he asked.

"Because you could be wrong," said Precious.

"But I'm not," said Sepo.

CHAPTER FIVE

T HAT NIGHT, as Precious lay on her sleeping mat, waiting for her father to come in and tell her a story – as he always did – she thought about what had happened at school. She did not like the thought of there being a thief at school – thieves spoiled everything: they made people suspicious of one another, which was not a good thing at all. People should be able to trust other people, without worrying about whether they would steal their possessions.

But even if she did not like the thought of there being a thief, neither did she like the thought that an innocent person might be suspected. She did not know the boy whom

41

Sepo had pointed out – she had seen him, of course, and she knew his name, Poloko (PO-LOW-KO), but she did not know very

PO·LOW·KO

much about him. And she certainly did not know that he was a thief.

This is Poloko.

You'll see that he was a rather round boy. If you saw walking along the street, you might think that perhaps that was a boy who ate a little bit too much. And if you got to know him a bit better, then you might be sure that this was so and that those bulges in his pockets were indeed sweets – a large number of them. But just because somebody has lots of sweets does *not* mean  that he has stolen them. One thing, you see, does not always lead to another. That is something that all detectives learn very early in their career, and Precious had already learned it. And she was only seven.

The next day at school, when they were copying out letters from the board, Sepo, who was sitting on the bench next to Precious, whispered, "Have you told anybody about the thief?"

Precious shook her head. "We don't know who it is. How can I tell the teacher about something I don't know?"

Sepo looked cross. "But *I* know who it is," he said. "And Big Mma Molipi told me that somebody has stolen three iced buns from her kitchen! She told me that this morning. Poloko's probably eaten them already!"

Precious listened in silence. She thought it a very unfair thing to say and she was about to tell Sepo that when the teacher gave them a severe look. So Precious just said, "Shh!" instead and left it at that. But later, when the children were let out to play while the teachers drank their tea,

Sepo and Tapiwa came up to her and said they wanted to speak to her.

"Are you going to help us deal with the thief?" Tapiwa said.

Precious tried to look surprised. She knew what they meant, but she did not want to help them without any proof. "I don't know what you're talking about," she said. "How can we deal with the thief if we don't know who it is?"

"But we do know," said Sepo. "It's Poloko, that's who it is."

Precious stared at Sepo. "You don't know that," she said. "So I'm not going to help you until you have some proof."

Sepo smiled. "All right," he said. "If you want some proof, we'll get it for you. We're going to look at his hands."

Precious wondered what he meant by that, but before she had the time to ask him, Sepo and Tapiwa ran off to the other side of the playground where they had seen Poloko sitting on a rock. Precious ran behind them – not because she wanted to help them, but because she wanted to see what was happening.

"Hold out your hands," Tapiwa said to Poloko. "Come on. Hold them out."

Poloko was surprised, but held out his hands. Tapiwa bent down to examine them. After a few moments, she pointed out something to Sepo, and he also bent down to look. Then Tapiwa reached out to feel Poloko's hands.

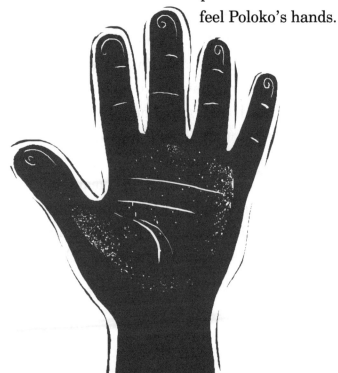

"Hah!" she shouted. "It's just as we thought. Your hands are sticky!"

Poloko tried to say something, but his words were drowned by the shouts of Tapiwa and Sepo. "Thief!" they cried out. "Thief! Thief!" It was a shrill cry, and it froze Precious's blood just to hear it. She wondered what it would be like to hear somebody shout that out about you – especially if you were not a thief and never had been.

Precious stood quite still.

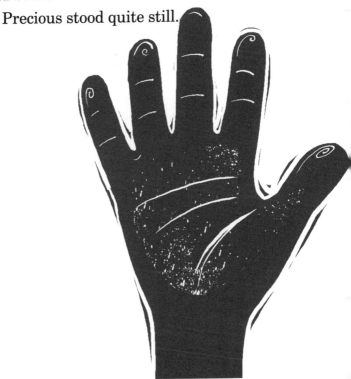

The others were now making such a noise that one of the teachers had been alerted and was coming to see what was wrong.

"What's all this noise?" the teacher asked. "Can't you children play quietly?"

"We've found the thief," Tapiwa shouted. "Look, Mma, look! His hands are covered in stickiness. If you want to know where those iced buns are, they're right there – in Poloko's stomach!"

CHAPTER SIX

THE TEACHER FROWNED. "What's all this?" she asked. "Are you children fighting?"

The two accusers were quick to deny this. "We're not fighting, Mma," cried Tapiwa, pointing a finger at Poloko. "We've found the thief. It's this boy! This boy right here!"

The teacher looked at Poloko. "Have you stolen something, Poloko?"

Poloko hung his head. "No, Mma, I have not stolen anything."

The teacher turned to stare at Tapiwa and Sepo. "Why do you say he's a thief?"

"Because some iced buns have been stolen," Sepo blurted out. "And his hands are sticky. Look at them, Mma!"

The teacher sighed. "Lots of people have sticky hands," she said. "That doesn't mean to say that they're thieves." She paused, looking down at Poloko. "You're sure you haven't stolen anything, Poloko?"

The boy was close to crying. "I have not stolen anything, Mma. I promise you."

The teacher shook a finger at Tapiwa and Sepo. "You be careful about accusing people of things when you have no proof," she said. "Now everybody go off and play and no more trouble, please."

Tapiwa and Sepo walked off, but only after throwing a disapproving look at Poloko. It was the sort of look that said *You're still a thief, you know.* And Poloko, who was clearly feeling very miserable, walked off in the other direction.

Precious waited for a moment before following the dejected-looking boy. "Poloko," she said, as she caught up with him. "I believe you. I don't think you're a thief."

He stopped. "Thank you, Precious. I know you don't think that." He paused, looking over his shoulder to where other children were standing, listening to Tapiwa and Sepo. "But they'll all think I'm a thief."

Precious knew that what he said was true. But she did not like to think that he was still unhappy, and so she tried to comfort him further. "It doesn't matter what people like that think," she said. "What matters is what your friends think. I'm your friend, and I know that you're telling the truth."

He listened to what she said and was about to say something when the bell sounded for them to return to the classroom. So he simply muttered "Thank you" and left it at that.

But Precious was not going to leave it there. That afternoon, when all the children left the school and began to walk back home under the hot African sun, she found Poloko and asked him to walk with her. They were going in the same direction, as he did not live far away from her.

He was pleased that she asked, as they could both see the other children looking at him suspiciously.

"You see," he said. "They've told everybody. Now they all think I'm a thief."

"Pay no attention to them," said Precious. "They can think what they like."

She knew, though, that it was not that simple. All of us worry about what other people think, even if we do not have to. It was easy to tell somebody to ignore that sort of thing; it was much harder to put such advice into practice.

They set off, following the path that wound down the hill. It was a narrow path and a winding one – here and there great boulders had rolled down the hill thousands of years ago and the path had to twist around these. In between the boulders, trees had grown up, their roots working their way through gaps in the stone. These trees made the places in between the rocks a cool refuge from the heat of the sun, and sometimes Precious would sit down there and rest on her way home. But these places were also good hiding places for snakes, and so you had to be careful or …

There was a noise off among the rocks, and they both gave a start.

"A snake?" whispered Poloko.

"Perhaps," said Precious. "Should we look?"

Poloko nodded. "Yes, but we must be careful."

They heard the noise again. This time Precious thought that it might be coming from the tree, and she looked up into the branches.

"There!" she said, pointing into the tangle of leaves.

Poloko looked up. He had expected to see a snake wound round one of the branches,

but that was not what he spotted.

"Monkeys!" he said.

Precious smiled. "They were watching us."

And then, just as she spoke, one of the monkeys dropped something. It fell down from the tree, caught in a shaft of light through the leaves. Poloko watched it, and then ran forward to pick it up, paying no heed to the excited chattering of the monkeys above his head.

For a moment or two he stared at it before passing it to Precious.

It was a piece of iced bun.

OW SHE WAS SURE. But it was one thing to be sure about something and quite another to prove it to others. That was something that all detectives knew, and although she had only just started being a detective, Precious was well aware that you had to be able to show people something if you wanted them to believe it.

That night, as she lay on her sleeping mat, she went over in her mind what she had seen. The monkeys were the culprits – they had given themselves away – but it would not be easy to catch them in the act. Monkeys were very nimble, and, in their own, special monkeyish way, very cunning.

It was much easier to catch a human being red-handed than to catch a monkey.

Red-handed … It was just an expression, a couple of words that meant to catch somebody in the middle of doing something wrong, but it was a good way of putting it and … red-handed?

She closed her eyes and imagined how monkeys would steal buns. They would dart in through the window when nobody was looking and their little hands, so like human hands in every respect, but a bit hairier, would stretch out and snatch. Those little hands … What if the thing they were trying to snatch was even stickier than the stickiest of iced buns? What if it was a cake filled with … icing sugar and GLUE?

Like all good ideas, it was enough to make you sit bolt upright. And that is what Precious did, sitting up on her sleeping mat, her eyes wide, a broad smile on her

face. Yes! She had worked out how to trap a thief, particularly one with tiny hands!

She lay down and closed her eyes again. It took some time for her to drop off, as it often does when one has had a particularly clever idea, but eventually she became drowsier and drowsier and went off to sleep.

She dreamed, and of course her dreams were about monkeys. She was walking under some trees in her dream and the monkeys were up in the branches above her. They were calling out, and to her

surprise they were calling her name. *Come up here, Precious. Come up here and join us.*

In your dreams you can often do things that you just cannot do when you are awake. Precious could not normally climb trees very well, but in her dream she could. It was very easy, in fact, and within moments she was up in the branches with the monkeys. They gathered about her, their tiny, wizened faces filled with joy at finding a new friend. Soft, tiny hands touched her, stroking her gently, while other hands explored her ears and hair.

Then they took her by the hand and led her along one of the branches. The ground was far away below, so hard and rocky if you should fall. *Don't be frightened*, said one of the monkeys. *It's very easy, you know.*

And with that, Precious began to swing from branch to branch, just as the

monkeys do. It was the most wonderful, light feeling, and her heart soared as she moved effortlessly through the canopy of leaves. So this was what it was like to live in the trees – it was like living in the sky. And it was like flying too. As she let go of one branch and swung through the air to another, she felt as light as one of the leaves itself might feel as it dropped from the bough.

She moved through the trees, the monkeys all about her, waving to her, encouraging her. And then slowly the trees thinned out and she was on the ground again. She looked for her friends, the monkeys, and saw that they were gone. So it is with dreams: they take us to places we cannot stay; they bring us friends who will soon be gone. That is the way it is with dreams.

THE NEXT MORNING, Precious was the first in the house to get out of bed. She had work to do – detective work – and her first task was to bake a cake. This was not difficult, as she was a good cook and had a well-tried recipe for sponge cake. Precious had learned to cook because she had to – her mother had died when she was very small and although her father thought that he was looking after her, when it came to cooking meals it was Precious who looked after him!

The cake did not take long, and was soon out of the oven. It smelled delicious, but she resisted the temptation to cut a slice for herself and try it. Rather than do that, she took a knife and cut out the middle of the cake so that it was left with a large hole in it.

The next bit of the plan was more difficult. Her father had a workshop next to the house – a place where he fixed fence posts and did odd carpentry jobs for friends. On a shelf in this workshop was a large pot of glue that he used for sticking wood together – it was very strong glue, a thick, sticky paste that was just the thing she was looking for.

Very carefully, making sure to get none on her fingers, Precious ladled out several spoonfuls of this glue onto a plate. Replacing the glue-pot on the shelf, she went back to the kitchen. Now she took the piece of cake that she had cut from the centre and mixed it up with the glue. It made a wonderfully sticky mess – just what she wanted.

She next put this sticky mixture back into the hole in the cake and covered the whole thing with icing. For good measure, she stuck a few red and yellow jelly sweets on the top. Nobody would be able to resist such a cake, she thought. Certainly no monkey would.

"That's a nice cake you've cooked," said her father over breakfast. "Is that for your teacher?"

Precious smiled. "No, I don't think so." She could imagine what would happen if the teacher ate that particular cake.

"For your friends?" asked her father.

Precious thought for a moment. She remembered her dream and the way the monkeys in it had welcomed her to their trees. Yes, they were her friends, she thought. In spite of all their tricks and their mischievousness, they were her friends.

She carried the cake to school in a box. When she arrived, she put the box down carefully and took out its mouth-watering contents.

"Look at that cake!" shouted somebody.

"Don't leave it there," said another. "If you leave it there, Precious, then Poloko will be sure to steal it!"

Other children laughed at this, but Precious did not. "Don't say that," she said crossly. But they did, and they said it again.

"Poloko will eat that entirely up," said one of the boys. "That's why he's so fat. He's a fat thief!"

Precious hoped that Poloko had not heard this, but feared that he had. She saw him walking away, his head lowered. People are so unkind, she thought. How would they like to be called a thief? Well, she would show them just how wrong they were.

With the cake left outside, on the shelf where the children left their bags, school began. Precious went into the classroom and tried to concentrate on the lesson that the teacher was giving, but it was not easy.

Her mind kept wandering, and she found herself imagining what was going on outside. The cake would be sitting there, the perfect temptation for any passing monkey, and it could only be a question of time before …

It happened suddenly. One moment everything was quiet, and the next there came a great squealing sound from outside. The squealing became louder and was soon a sort of howling sound, rather like the siren of a fire engine.

The teacher and the entire class looked up in astonishment.

"What on earth is going on?" asked the teacher. "Open the door, Sepo, and see what's happening."

The entire class took this as an invitation to go to the door, and they were soon all gathered round the open door and the windows too, peering out to see what was going on.

What was happening was that two
monkeys were dancing up and down
alongside the shelf, their hands stuck firmly
in the mixture of glue and cake. Struggle
as they might to free themselves, each time
they withdrew a hand it came out with a
long strand of glue that dragged it back
in. They were thoroughly and completely
stuck to the cake.

"See," shouted Precious in triumph.
"There are the thieves, Mma. See there!"

The teacher laughed. "Well, well. So it's
monkeys who have been up to no good.
Well, well!"

The school gardener had been alerted to the sound of squealing, and he now appeared. Seizing the monkeys, he pulled them away from the cake, freeing them to scamper back to the trees not far away.

"Little rascals," he shouted, shaking a fist at them as they disappeared.

The teacher called everybody back to their desks. "We shall have to be more careful in future," she said. "Don't leave anything out to tempt those monkeys. That's the way to deal with that."

Precious said nothing.

Then the teacher continued. "And I hope that some of you have learned a lesson," she said. "Those who accused Poloko of being a thief may like to think about what they have just seen."

The teacher looked at Sepo and Tapiwa, who both looked down at the floor. Precious watched them. They had learned a lesson, she thought.

On the way back from school that day, Poloko came up to her and thanked her for what she had done. "You are a very kind girl," he said. "Thank you."

"That's all right," she said.

"You're going to be a very good detective one day," he went on. "Do you still want to be one?"

She thought for a moment. It was a good thing to be a detective. You could help people who needed help. You could fight injustice. You could make people happier – as Poloko now was.

"Yes," she said. "I think I do."

They walked on. In the trees not far away, there were some small eyes watching them from the leaves. The monkeys. Her friends.

Poloko walked back past her house, and Precious turned to him and said, "Would you like me to make a cake? We could eat it for our tea?"

He said he would, and while Precious baked the cake, he sat outside and sniffed the delicious smell wafting through the kitchen window.

Then the cake was ready, and they each had a large slice.

"Perfect," said Poloko. "First class, number one cake."

And that is when she thought *When I have a detective agency I'll call it the No. 1 Ladies' Detective Agency*.

Many years later, she did just that. Which shows something else: when you decide that you want to do something, really want to do it, then you can. You really can.